The Secret of Spooky House

Story by Joy Cowley

In Spooky House,
the Monster family was at the table.
Mr. and Mrs. Monster
were having supper.
The Monster child
was having a tantrum.

"Beetles! Beetles! Beetles!"
she screamed.
"I'm sick of boiled beetles!
I want popcorn!"

"Stop!" said Mr. Monster.
"You're making my blood curdle."

3

"Why can't I have popcorn?"
cried the Monster child.

"Because we don't eat popcorn,"
said Mrs. Monster.
"Monsters have never eaten popcorn.
We don't even say that word."

4

"Here, my little pet,"
said Mr. Monster.
"Try some fried mice!"

"I don't want fried mice!"
the Monster child screamed.
"I want popcorn."

5

Mrs. Monster went to the kitchen
and came back again.

"Look what I have for you!"
she said to the Monster child.
"A yummy mud pie
and a glass of caterpillar juice!"

The Monster child
threw the food and the drink
at the wall.
"Popcorn, popcorn, popcorn!"

7

Mr. and Mrs. Monster whispered.

"What's wrong with her?"
said Mr. Monster.

"She's not sick," said Mrs. Monster.

"What I'd like to know is —
where does she get
her strange tastes from?"
said Mr. Monster.

The Monster child was still screaming.
"What will we do?" said Mrs. Monster.

Mr. Monster whispered in her ear,
"I'm afraid I'll have to go out
and buy her some popcorn."

9

Mr. Monster put on dark glasses.
He hid himself in a hat
and a big cloak.
Then he went to the all-night shop.

The man in the shop
didn't have popcorn,
but he did have corn to pop.

Mr. Monster bought six packets
and tiptoed home.

11

The Monster child stopped crying
as soon as the corn began to pop.

Pop, pop, pop!

Mr. Monster looked in the pan.
He thought he would try
just one little piece.

Crunch, crunch — yum!

"Come quickly, my dear!"
Mr. Monster yelled to his wife.
"Dig your fangs into this!
It's delicious!"

The Monster family
thought popcorn was so good
that they bought sacks full of corn
and popped it every night.

Every night,
strange noises
came from Spooky House.
Pop, pop, pop!
Crunch, crunch, crunch!

"I hope the neighbors
never find out," said Mr. Monster.

16